D0131312

Shawn's Window

By William Perdue

Illustrated by Serena Lopez

gatekeeper press
Columbus, Ohio

Shawn's Window

Published by Gatekeeper Press

2167 Stringtown Rd, Suite 109

Columbus, OH 43123-2989

www.GatekeeperPress.com

ISBN (hardcover): 9781662900488

Shawn's Window

By William Perdue

Shawn's teacher, Mrs. Rush, explained to her class, "Today, we are going to draw a picture."

But Shawn was staring out the classroom window.

"Shawn, PLEASE pay attention. I promise, your parents will be back to pick you up after school."

"Boys and girls, your picture must explain who you are. My example is on the board."

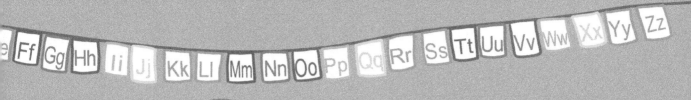

"Shawn, I know you want to be on the other side of that window. If you listen, and do your work, you can play basketball during recess."

"Class, I want you to shine like the stars you are. So make sure your pictures have delightful colors."

"Shawn, I'm sorry to be a helicopter teacher, but if you don't finish your work, I'm afraid you will be stuck inside this classroom all day."

"Okay, students. Hand in your perfect pictures, please."

"OH, SHAWN! What a beautiful picture you've drawn. You're such a shooting star! I'm proud to see you were paying attention the whole time."

CPSIA information can be obtained
at www.ICGtesting.com
Printed in the USA
LVHW071504210820
663836LV00020B/203

9 781662 900488